SEE NO EVIL

Story by Emmett Davis
Illustrations by Jenny Franz

A Carnival Press Book   Raintree Publishers Inc.

*The spirit of adventure and the sense of community of **See No Evil** are dedicated by the author to Gaye Doeden and Mary Neuenfeldt.*

The artist dedicates this book to Robin and Bruce, with thanks.

Published by Raintree Publishers Inc., 205 West Highland Avenue, Milwaukee, Wisconsin 53203.

Art Direction: Su Lund

Printed in the United States of America.   1 2 3 4 5 6 7 8 9 0 87 86 85 84 83

Library of Congress Cataloging in Publication Data
Davis, Emmett A., 1948-   See no evil.   "A Carnival Press book."
Summary: In attempting to observe macaques in their natural setting in the mountains of Japan, Sumiko and Yukio experience some frightening moments.   [1. Japanese macaque—Fiction.   2. Monkeys—Fiction.
3. Japan—Fiction]   I. Franz, Jenny, ill.   II. Title.
PZ7.D2883Se   1983   [Fic]   83-8609   ISBN 0-940742-14-4

Saru-san, my art teacher Mr. Izue
asked me to make this diary entry after
I searched for you and your people,
the snow monkeys.

Three days ago I arrived at my
Uncle Joji's farm in the shadow of your
mountain Gorin-zan. I have always
wanted to draw the snow monkeys—
to really capture their spirit as the artist
Okatome did over a century ago in his
netsuke statue.

I will never forget this visit . . . .

"Sumiko, please draw another picture."

"Enough, Yukio!" I closed my sketch pad. "Tell me more about the macaques. Why haven't we seen them?"

"The monkeys are wild and travel where they will," explained Aunt Kiku. "But you two are not wild, so go gather some eggs for me."

We picked up empty baskets and went outside.

On the way back to the house, Yukio stopped me. "Cousin Sumiko, can't you stay just one day longer? Taro, the village hunter, says the snow monkeys stay in the valley east of Gorin-zan." He pointed to the area. "I'm certain they will leave the valley and search here for food tomorrow. Then I can show you the mother and baby that come right up to me."

"We'll see, Cousin. You've just given me an idea."

"Tell me!" he begged.

"Oh, nothing. Come on. We should hurry back with the eggs."

Very early in the morning, I slipped from beneath my warm quilt, dressing quietly so I wouldn't wake Yukio. Snatching my leather bag of art materials, I eased myself out the back door.

Outside, I pulled on my boots. The gate behind Aunt Kiku's vegetable garden creaked loudly enough to wake the whole valley. But no lights went on in the farmhouse. I walked through Taro's radish fields near the forest.

Saru-san! The spruce trees were dark and massive. In the moonlight, I tried to find a path through the woods. "Should I go back?" I wondered.

"Sumiko. Stop!"

I froze, terrified at being discovered. Suddenly, Yukio ran up beside me.

"Ah, I knew you would try this," he scolded me, "so I packed sleeping bags and food for us *and* the snow monkeys."

I scrunched up my face at him for frightening me. But, with his face beaming up at me, I felt warmer and more sure of myself.

Eager to be off, Yukio ran ahead. "Come over here to Taro's path," he called.

I followed silently.

Taro's trail ended in a stand of pine trees, carpeted with a bed of slippery old needles.

Clouds hid the moon. The wind picked up, bringing snow. We stumbled over rocks along a small stream, no longer sure where we were going.

"The storm's getting worse," I shouted. "We'll have to stop."

Shivering, we unpacked Yukio's bundle beneath the shelter of a rock ledge and burrowed inside our bedrolls. Snow swirled all around us.

The howling wind gradually calmed, but the sky stayed dark.

"Look," said Yukio, pointing. "There's a fox down by the stream bed. Old Kitsune will bring us bad luck!"

"Don't talk like that, Yukio."

"Many say it's true. The mountains are filled with dangers like evil Kitsune."

The fox moved closer to our hiding place. Suddenly—"Kiak! Kiak! Kiak!" The trees around us came to life with cries of warning.

The fox was as startled by the noise as we were. He disappeared into the forest. But what had made the sounds?

"Snow monkeys, Sumiko. We've found their night camp!"

Delighted, I stood up, pulling on my boots. My sudden movements scared some of the monkeys. I stood quietly, not wanting to lose them now.

"Throw them some food," I whispered.

Yukio pulled out some sweet potatoes and tossed them toward the macaques.

Most of the monkeys huddled in the trees, but an old, bearded fellow climbed slowly down to meet us. I carefully pulled an apple from Yukio's bundle and offered it to him.

Just two feet away from me, the leader of the troop stood on his hind legs, his head level with my belt. His eyes shifted back and forth between me and the apple. After a minute, he majestically took the red fruit, turned, and walked back to his tree.

"Good!" Yukio said. "The snow monkeys will stay near us now. Perhaps they'll show us the way home."

The wind blew strongly again, but I was too excited to think about the cold. Grabbing my pens and sketch pad, I drew several babies clinging to their mothers. Older monkeys scampered around us, pushing, tumbling, and chasing.

Adults paired off to groom, one monkey fingering the fur of another. I laughed as I sketched them, remembering how Mother used to scratch and rub *my* back.

"Sumiko, here's a hot spring," my cousin called. I joined him by the steaming pool. It was a tight fit, but three monkeys were soaking together. Their fluffy fur, powdered with snow, became wet and matted.

23

Snowflakes began to fall. I was worried about getting trapped in another storm, but Yukio had found his mother and baby monkey.

They reminded me of the trio "Hear No Evil, Speak No Evil, See No Evil." I sketched them from a distance.

As I completed my drawings, the leader cried out, "Kya! Kya!" Everything stopped as the troop answered, "Hui! Hui! Hui!" Then the monkeys began to move out to hunt for food.

We were suddenly left behind. "Quickly, Yukio, we must pack!"

Yukio and I hurried through the deepening snow. Finally, we caught up with the monkeys and stayed with the troop. Thoroughly lost, I prayed that they were not heading deeper into the mountains.

All of a sudden, a monkey guard and then the leader warned, "Kiak! Kiak! Kiak!" The entire troop left us behind once again as some monkeys ran uphill and others swung from tree to tree. Something dangerous was coming.

Through the branches, we spotted dark figures moving toward us. "Come back!" Yukio called out for the monkeys. But all his shouting did was bring the figures closer.

"It's Kitsune!" yelled Yukio.

"Yukio!"

"Sumiko!"

It wasn't a fox after all! It was Uncle Joji and Taro. Uncle swung Yukio up in his arms, hugging and scolding him. Taro poured us hot tea as we told them about the snow monkeys.

Feeling much warmer, we headed back to Uncle Joji's farmhouse. Aunt Kiku met us at the door. There were more hugs and scoldings for us. A hot bath was our punishment, and a hot breakfast was our reward.

Actually, Saru-san, my reward will be memories. Memories of Yukio and his family. Memories of your snow monkeys and the harsh beauty of your mountain.

My drawings will always remind me of my search for you.

Sumiko's adventure took place in a central district of Honshu, one of the four main islands of *Japan*. Farmers have lived there for centuries next to wilderness areas of steep tree-covered mountains. The area is dotted with hot springs, reminders of ancient volcanoes. Bear, fox, deer, and monkeys make their homes in the forests.

The monkeys, or macaques, live in troops of thirty to sixty under the leadership of a single male. Often called *snow monkeys*, they are the only monkeys outside of zoos that live so far north in the world. The Japanese government protects the macaques, but the monkeys' territory is steadily shrinking as more and more wilderness land is developed by people. Sumiko's writing in this book is directly addressed to the monkeys. (*Saru* or *Saru-san* is the Japanese term for monkey).

Monkeys have been found in Japanese stories and artwork for hundreds of years. One form of Japanese art often used for the monkeys is the *netsuke*, tiny carvings of wood or ivory.

Author **Emmett Davis** says, "Everybody should write a book, for birthing a book is less the record of a journey than a journey itself. Spinning a tale creates a company as full of fellow pilgrims as any going to Canterbury in Aprille." This is one of several children's books by the author.

Jenny Franz spent much of her childhood drawing and painting. After receiving fine arts training and ad agency experience, she settled in the Midwest with her husband and all her art materials. Ms. Franz is the illustrator of several books for children.